GUESS
HOW MUCH
I LOVE YOU

To Liz with love,
A.J.

First U.S. edition 1995

Library of Congress Cataloging-in-Publication Data

McBratney, Sam.
Guess how much I love you / by Sam McBratney ; illustrated by
Anita Jeram. — 1st U.S. ed.

Summary: During a bedtime game, every time Little Nutbrown
Hare demonstrates how much he loves his father, Big Nutbrown
Hare gently shows him that the love is returned even more.
ISBN 1-56402-473-3 (reinforced trade ed.)
[1. Hares—Fiction. 2. Fathers and sons—Fiction. 3. Bedtime—
Fiction. 4. Love—Fiction.] I. Jeram, Anita, ill. II. Title.
PZ7.M47826Gu   1995
[E]—dc20   94-1599

30 29 28 27 26 25

Printed in Italy

The pictures in this book were done in pen and ink and watercolor.

Candlewick Press
2067 Massachusetts Avenue
Cambridge, Massachusetts 02140

GUESS
HOW MUCH
I LOVE YOU

by
Sam McBratney

illustrated by
Anita Jeram

CANDLEWICK PRESS
CAMBRIDGE, MASSACHUSETTS

Little Nutbrown Hare,
who was going to bed, held
on tight to Big Nutbrown Hare's
very long ears.

He wanted to be sure that Big
Nutbrown Hare was listening.
"Guess how much
I love you," he said.

"Oh, I don't think I could guess that,"
said Big Nutbrown Hare.

"This much," said Little
Nutbrown Hare, stretching out
his arms as wide as they could go.

Big Nutbrown Hare had even
longer arms. "But I love *you*
this much," he said.

Hmm, that is a lot, thought
Little Nutbrown Hare.

"I love you
as high as
I can reach,"
said Little
Nutbrown
Hare.

"I love you as high as *I* can reach," said Big Nutbrown Hare.

That is very
high, thought
Little Nutbrown
Hare. I wish
I had arms
like that.

Then Little
Nutbrown Hare
had a good idea.
He tumbled
upside down
and reached
up the tree
trunk with
his feet.

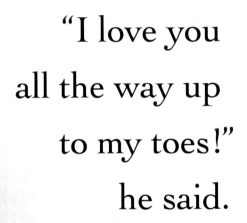

"I love you
all the way up
to my toes!"
he said.

"And *I* love you
all the way up
to your toes," said
Big Nutbrown Hare,
swinging him up
over his head.

"I love you
   as high as
   I can hop!"
      laughed Little
         Nutbrown Hare,

bouncing up

      and down.

"But I love you as high as
I can hop," smiled Big
Nutbrown Hare—and he
hopped so high that his ears
touched the branches above.

That's good
hopping,
thought
Little
Nutbrown
Hare.
I wish I
could hop
like that.

"I love you all the way down the
lane as far as the river," cried
Little Nutbrown Hare.

"I love you across the river
and over the hills," said
Big Nutbrown Hare.

That's very far, thought
Little Nutbrown Hare.

He was almost too sleepy
to think anymore.

Then he looked beyond the
thornbushes, out into the big
dark night. Nothing could
be farther than the sky.

"I love you right up to the moon," he said, and closed his eyes.

"Oh, that's far," said Big Nutbrown Hare. "That is very, very far."

Big Nutbrown Hare settled
Little Nutbrown Hare
into his bed of leaves.

He leaned over
and kissed him
good night.

Then he lay down close by
and whispered with a smile,
"I love you right up to the moon—

and back."